JACK RUSSELL:
Dog Detective

The Sausage
Situation

JACK RUSSELL: Dog Detective

The Sausage
Situation

DARREL & SALLY ODGERS

Kane Miller
A DIVISION OF EDC PUBLISHING

First American Edition 2007
by Kane/Miller Book Publishers, Inc.
La Jolla, California

Text copyright © Sally and Darrel Odgers, 2006
Cover design copyright © Lake Shore Graphics, 2006
Interior illustrations © Scholastic Australia, 2006
Cover photographs by Michael Bagnall
Dog, Frisbee, courtesy of the Cansick family
Interior illustrations by Janine Dawson

First published by Scholastic Australia Pty Limited in 2006
This edition published under license from Scholastic Australia Pty Limited.

All rights reserved. For information contact:
Kane/Miller Book Publishers, Inc.
P.O. Box 8515
La Jolla, CA 92038
www.kanemiller.com
www.edcpub.com
www.usbornebooksandmore.com

Library of Congress Control Number: 2007921057
Printed and bound in the United States of America
6 7 8 9 10 11 12 13 14 15

ISBN: 978-1-933605-54-8

Dear Readers,

The story you're about
to read is about me and my
friends, and how we sorted out The
Sausage Situation. To save time, I'll
introduce us all to you now. Of course,
if you know us already, you can trot off
to Chapter One.

I am Jack Russell, Dog Detective. I
live with my landlord, Sarge, in
Doggeroo. Sarge detects human-type
crimes. I have the important job of
detecting crimes that deal with dogs.
I'm a Jack Russell terrier, so I am
dogged and intelligent.

Next door to Sarge and me live
Auntie Tidge and Foxie. Auntie Tidge
is lovely. She has biscuits. Foxie is not
lovely. He's a fox terrier (more or less).

He used to be a street dog, and a thief, but he's reformed now. Auntie Tidge has even gotten rid of his fleas. Foxie sometimes helps me with my cases.

Uptown Lord Setter (Lord Red for short) lives in Uptown House with Caterina Smith. Lord Red means well, but he isn't very bright.

We have other friends and acquaintances in Doggeroo. These include Polly the dachshund, Jill Russell, the Squekes, Ralf Boxer and Shuffle the pug. Then there's Fat Molly Cat from the library.

That's all you need to know, so let's get on with Chapter One.

Yours doggedly,

Jack Russell – the detective with a nose for crime.

 Scenting Sausages

The Sausage Situation began on a day when crime was a long way from my mind.

I was thinking of something very important. Jill Russell's people had invited me to spend a few days at their place.

When Sarge came out to the porch, I did the **paw thing**. I was telling Sarge it was time to go to Jill Russell's.

"You're not coming with me today, Jack," said Sarge. "I'm going to the school to give a talk on road safety."

I rolled my eyes.

Jack's Facts

*All dogs know exactly how to make
their people feel guilty.
Nice dogs do this only when their
people deserve it.
I am a nice dog.
This is a fact.*

    "Sorry, Jack." Sarge patted my head.

    I sighed. Then I wagged my tail
five times, to show I forgave him.

    After Sarge had gone, I settled to
wait. After quite a while, I saw two
paws poking through a hole under
the hedge.

    "Who goes there?" I demanded.

    The paws **pawsed**.

    "I know it's you, Foxie," I said.

"Why are you sneaking around?"

Foxie **ig-gnawed** that. He came up onto my porch. "Auntie Tidge is cleaning the freezer in the kitchen. She sent me out. Let's go and visit Jill Russell."

"We can't go today, and you're not invited anyway," I said.

Foxie sulked. "Auntie Tidge planted some lettuce. Let's dig them up."

"That's no fun," I said. "You can't play with lettuce. You get grit in your teeth."

"You can always ... " Foxie stopped suddenly, and sniffed the air.

"What is it?" I asked.

Foxie sniffed harder and started to drool. He had scented something. I quickly made a **nose map**.

Jack's map:

1. *My empty dinner bowl.*

2. *Foxie.*

3. *A van.*

4. *Auntie Tidge.*

5. *Strange man.*

6. *Sausages.*

"Sausages!" said Foxie. He jumped up and scooted back to his own yard.

All dogs depend on their noses.
Jack Russells use their other senses as well.
This is why Jack Russells are **su-paw-rior**.
This is a fact.

The sausage scent was coming from the road outside Auntie Tidge's house.

I heard a door slam. That must be the van I had nose-mapped, I thought.

I heard the latch on Foxie's gate click open.

I heard a strange man speaking. "Here are your sausages, **Miss Russell**.

Where do you want them?"

"In the kitchen, Mr. Beale," said Auntie Tidge. "I'll put them in the freezer. Foxie-woxie, no! Down!"

I heard the strange man yell. I **jack-jumped** to look over the fence and saw he had tripped over Foxie.

The sausage scent was getting stronger.

"No, Foxie, no! *Bad* dog! No!" Auntie Tidge sounded upset.

We had a **situation** here. It was some kind of Sausage Situation. Auntie Tidge was in trouble!

Jack Russell's the name, detection's the game! I went to rescue her.

Auntie Tidge was sitting on her garden path with her legs stuck out in front of her. I **greeted** her to make sure she was all right. The strange man was yelling at Foxie.

There were boxes scattered on the ground. One had burst open. Foxie had his head right inside it, and I could hear him guzzling and gulping.

I didn't need a nose map to tell me Foxie was feasting on sausages.

Jack's Facts

Human-type food does not belong on the ground.
Therefore, eating human-type food that has fallen on the ground is not stealing.
It is cleaning up a mess.
This is a fact.

I was about to help Foxie clean up the mess when Sarge came up the path. He shut Foxie in the garden shed and sent me home.

Jack's Glossary

Paw thing. *Up on hind legs, paws held together as if praying. Means pleased excitement.*

Pawsed. *Stopped to think, done by a dog.*

Ig-gnawed. *Ignored, but done by dogs.*

Nose map. *Way of storing information collected by the nose.*

Su-paw-rior. *Superior, the way Jack Russells are.*

Jack's Glossary

Miss Russell. *I am Jack Russell. Sarge is Sergeant Russell. Auntie Tidge is Miss Russell.*

Jack-jump. *A sudden spring made by a Jack Russell terrier.*

Situation. *Something of interest to a dog detective.*

Greet. *This is done by rising to the hind legs and clutching a person with the paws while slurping them up the face.*

"Stop Thief"

Foxie was still grumbling about The Sausage Situation two days later.

"Those sausages were mine by right," he kept saying. "They were on the ground in my **terrier-tory**!"

"I know. You were guzzling them," I said.

"I only had three. Auntie Tidge hid the rest before she let me out of the shed."

"That's so you wouldn't eat them all at once and be sick." I was tired of hearing about The Sausage Situation. I had other things on my mind.

"Foxie-woxie! **Jackie-wackie!**" called Auntie Tidge from Foxie's house.

"She's going to give us sausages!" yelped Foxie. He shot home. I followed. Maybe Auntie Tidge was going to take me to Jill Russell's place? She takes me out sometimes, when Sarge is busy at work.

Auntie Tidge had the boxes of sausages stacked on the table. Even my **super-sniffer** had trouble detecting them, because they were so cold. They must have been stored in the freezer.

Auntie Tidge caught Foxie as he dashed past, and picked up a brush.

"Keep still, Foxie-woxie. I want to make you look smart." She leashed him to a chair leg, and brushed him smooth. Then she brushed me. She patted us and got up. "Wait here, boys. I have to pop 'round to Dora's before we go."

"Before we go *where*?" I asked Foxie when Auntie Tidge had gone out. "Are we going to Jill Russell's?"

Foxie ig-gnawed me. He was trying to climb up the leg of the table.

"Stop that," I said. "You'll have the whole lot of sausages on top of us."

"Good!" howled Foxie. "I will eat them *all*."

Above the noise Foxie was making, I heard a van stop outside.

I made a quick nose map.

Jack's map:

1. *Foxie.*

2. *Sausages.*

3. *Auntie Tidge.*

4. *Lord Red.*

5. *Caterina Smith.*

There was a knock on the door. "Cooee? Are you there, Auntie Tidge?" It was Caterina Smith. She knocked again, and then opened the door and came in.

Foxie ig-gnawed her, so I growled a warning.

Jack's Facts

It is a dog's duty to protect his terrier-tory. If a dog neglects his duty, his pal must do it for him.
Foxie was neglecting his duty.
This is a fact.

"Don't be silly, Jack," said Caterina Smith. She picked up the boxes of sausages and carried them out the door.

"She's stealing my sausages!"

yelped Foxie. "Stop her, Jack!"

Foxie was tied to the chair leg, so I leapt into action, and darted through the **dogdoor** in pursuit. I couldn't stop Caterina Smith, but I *could* follow her and **monitor this situation**.

Behind me, I heard a **terrier-able** noise. It was Foxie, dragging the chair behind him. He tried to get out the dogdoor behind me. There was an

even more terrier-able noise as the chair hit the door.

"Stop, thief!" bawled Foxie as I ran down the path and through the gate.

Caterina Smith's van was parked by the curb. She opened the side door, and slid the pile of boxes inside. I saw Lord Red peering out of the rear window. Was Lord Red an accessory to this crime? I could hardly believe it!

"Stop in the name of the paw!" I ordered. I grabbed Caterina Smith by the hem of her skirt and tugged. "Those are Auntie Tidge's sausages."

Caterina Smith looked down at me and frowned. "Back you go, Jack. I'm in a hurry." She pulled me off her skirt, put me back through the gate, and closed it behind me.

Of course, I didn't stay in the yard.

I got out (never mind how) just as
Caterina Smith drove away with the
sausages.

Jack's Glossary

Terrier-tory. *A territory owned
by a terrier.*

Jackie-wackie. *Auntie Tidge is
the only person allowed to call
me that.*

Super-sniffer. *Jack's nose in
super-sniff mode.*

Jack's Glossary

Dogdoor. *A door especially for dogs.*

Monitor this situation. *Keep close watch on something interesting.*

Terrier-able. *Same as terrible, but to do with terriers.*

 # FoLLow That Van

"Follow that van, detective!" I told myself. "Don't let the thief get away!"

I dashed in pursuit, but not even a tracking Jack can keep up with a van being driven by a sausage thief. Jacks are fast and fearless, but at last I began to fall behind.

I was about to give up and turn back when the van stopped. Caterina Smith got out, and picked me up.

"Bad dog, Jack! I wondered why Lordie was making such a fuss in the back. I can't leave you wandering around, so you'll just have to come with me."

I hoped she might put me with the boxes of stolen sausages, so I could go on monitoring the situation. Instead, she bundled me into the back seat with Lord Red.

Red was pawfully pleased to see me. He bounced around with excitement. His ears bounced too. "Jack, Jack, are you coming to the Dog and Sausage Day with me, Jack? Are you? Why isn't Foxie coming, Jack? Doesn't he want to … ?"

"Stop it, Red!" I snapped. "One thing at a time. Don't you realize I'm being **dognapped**?"

Red stopped bouncing. "Dognapped? Who's dognapping you?"

21

"Caterina Smith," I explained.

"Caterina Smith isn't a dognapper, Jack. Besides, why would she dognap you? She's already got a dog. She's got me."

"First she stole some sausages, and now she's dognapped me because I was tracking her."

"You're not being dognapped, Jack, and Caterina Smith hasn't stolen anything."

"I am, and she has," I said. "I'm on the trail of the stolen sausages. Caterina Smith has … "

"Don't be silly, Jack," said Red. "Caterina Smith is bringing the sausages to Dog and Sausage Day. That's where we're going right now."

"But … " I stopped. Suddenly I realized I might have gotten it wrong.

<u>Jack's Facts</u>

Any dog who thinks he is always right is often wrong.
A smart dog will admit that sooner rather than later.
Jack Russells are smart dogs.
This is a fact.

I considered the facts. Caterina Smith is Auntie Tidge's friend. Maybe Auntie Tidge had said she could have the sausages? Maybe we really were on our way to Dog and Sausage Day? I wasn't sure. All I could do was continue to monitor the situation.

"What's Dog and Sausage Day?" I asked.

"It happens at the friendly school," said Red. "It's even better fun than a show! There are chew toys, and ball games and a costume parade. Caterina Smith made me a costume. She says the kids will love me."

For the first time, I noticed Lord Red was wearing a tube of brown stretchy material. It reached all the way from his shoulders right back to his hind legs.

"What are you meant to be?" I asked. "A stocking?"

"I am dressed as a corn dog," said Red.

I was about to **in-terrier-gate** Red more, when the van stopped at the school.

People and dogs were everywhere. I saw Polly Smote with a ruffle around her neck. Shuffle the pug had a little hat.

Caterina Smith left us in the van while she carried the sausage boxes away.

I was worried.

Jacks jump over.

Jacks burrow under.

Jacks squeeze through.

But ... not even a Jack can escape from the back of a van.

How could I monitor the Sausage Situation from here?

Jack's Glossary

Dognapped. *Like kidnapped, but done to a dog.*

In-terrier-gate. *Official questioning, done by a terrier.*

Doggeroo Dog and Sausage Day

While I was still worrying, Auntie Tidge's little car pulled up behind us. The windows were closed, but I could hear Foxie nagging Auntie Tidge about the sausages. When he saw me in the van, he almost jumped through the windshield.

"I'll get you for this, Jack Russell!"

"What's wrong with Foxie?" asked Red.

"He thinks we've got those sausages," I said.

Auntie Tidge let Foxie out. Foxie dashed to the van, and jumped up and down.

"Sausages! Sausages! Sausages!" he yapped.

That was a mistake. All the other dogs had been trotting around with their people. When they heard what Foxie was yapping, they joined in.

The three Squekes had been yaffling around with their person, Dora Barkins. Then they heard Foxie.

"Sausages? Sausages! Where? Where? Where?" they yaffled.

Polly **dached** up next. "Sausages? Did someone say sausages?" she demanded.

"Sausages!" Shuffle joined in.

Even Ralf Boxer, who is hardly as big as a sausage himself, started yapping.

Lord Red joined in. "Sausages! Sausages!"

Since I was shut in the van with him, his voice sounded terrier-ably loud.

"Stop that, Red!" I yelped.

Red stopped. The other dogs didn't. Their people started shouting.

Auntie Tidge grabbed Foxie.

"Sausages!" barked Foxie, leaping at the van again.

"They're not here!" I barked back. "We have a new situation! Caterina Smith took them away!"

"Where? Where?" Foxie pulled away from Auntie Tidge. "Someone's stealing my sausages again!" He darted off. Auntie Tidge let him go. She is not the right shape for running.

She let me and Lord Red out of the van. "*There* you are, Jackie-wackie! I wish you wouldn't disappear like that. And now Foxie's done it too. I don't know what's gotten into him today."

I knew. Three sausages and a big idea had gotten into Foxie. That was the trouble!

Caterina Smith came back without the sausages.

"All the dogs are being silly," said Auntie Tidge. "Jack and Lordie are the only ones who remember their manners."

I greeted Auntie Tidge for that. Then I got down to business. I had to find Foxie before he did something terrier-able.

I made a nose map.

Jack's map:

1. Lots of dogs.

2. Lots of people.

3. Auntie Tidge.

4. Lord Red.

5. Caterina Smith.

6. Foxie.

7. Sausages.

8. Onions.

The sausage scent was faint. So was the Foxie scent. The onion scent was strong. It all seemed to be coming from a green tent. I set off across the schoolyard to investigate. Dogs had been playing ball games with kids. Now they were all racing around hunting for sausages instead.

I'd almost reached the green tent when Sarge called.

"Jack? Jack, come back here!"

Mostly, when Sarge calls, I answer. It might be time for dinner, or a ball game. It might be time to visit Jill Russell.

This time, I ig-gnawed Sarge. I raced around the side of the green tent. People and dogs scattered as I ran. I was a Jack on a mission.

I *had* to catch up with Foxie.

I stopped so suddenly that my paws skidded on the grass.

Why did I have to catch up with Foxie?

I sat down and shook my ears. Why should I monitor the Sausage Situation? They weren't *my* sausages. Auntie Tidge must have said Caterina Smith could take them. If Foxie was going to be terrier-able, why should *I* get involved?

I trotted back to Sarge.

Jack's Glossary

Dached. *The way dachshunds get around.*

 Seeking Sausages

"Hello, Jack," said Sarge. He patted me. "Auntie says Foxie has upset all the dogs and run off."

I **jack-attacked** Sarge's leg to get attention, and **pointed** towards the green tent.

"Over there, eh?" asked Sarge. "Trust Foxie to follow the food." He looked at barking dogs and scolding people, and lifted his voice. "Control your dogs!"

Everyone did as Sarge said.

<u>*Jack's Facts*</u>

Sarge is a police sergeant.
Police sergeants are like Jack Russell
terriers.
When they give orders, people and dogs
obey.
This is a fact.

Inside the tent, there was a table
stacked with sausage boxes. Jack and
Jill Johnson from the station were
cooking onions and buttering bread.

I sneezed. Then I remembered
something. Where was Jill Russell? I
couldn't believe I'd forgotten her. Jack
and Jill Johnson were Jill Russell's
people. So, why wasn't she here?

I went to Jack Johnson. I did the

paw thing. Then I did the paw thing
to Jill Johnson. I whined.

Jill Johnson laughed. "Jill Russell
couldn't come today, Jack. She's safer
at home." She waved her cooking
tongs at Polly, who had followed us
in. "Off you go, Polly. Onions are bad
for dogs."

Polly snorted. "I don't want
onions," she told me. "Why would I
want onions? I want those sausages."

I looked up at the boxes. I looked
down at Polly. Her legs were too short
for her to jump up there.

"Go *away!*" Jill Johnson waved her
tongs again.

The three Squekes yaffled through
the door. "Sausages, sausages,
sausages!" They all wore little striped
jackets. They looked like hairy wasps.

"Boys? Boys!" Dora Barkins dashed in and scooped them up. "*So* sorry," she said.

"Don't worry, Dora. Half the dogs in Doggeroo have been seeking sausages in here. Somehow, they know what's in those boxes." Jill Johnson wagged her tongs at a bonehead wearing a bonnet. It had burrowed under the back flap of the tent.

"Have you seen Foxie?" asked Sarge. "Auntie is worried about him. My Jack seemed to think he was here."

"No," said Jill Johnson. "Your Jack just wants to see Jill Russell, or maybe eat sausages. Which is it, Jackie-wackie?"

I like Jill Johnson, but Auntie Tidge is the *only* person allowed to call me that.

I left the tent. Caterina Smith wasn't a thief or a dognapper, but now I had a mystery to solve.

Where *was* Foxie? I sat down and tried to make a nose map.

All I could smell was onions. With my super-sniffer out of action, I used my other senses. I got up on my hind legs and looked around. I jack-jumped. I saw plenty of dogs. I saw three fox terriers. None was Foxie.

I pricked my ears. Most dogs had stopped barking. People talked and laughed. Birds twittered. Squekes yaffled. I heard Sarge say goodbye to Jack and Jill Johnson. I couldn't hear Foxie.

"Jack, Jack!" Red charged across the grass. "What's going on, Jack?"

"I'm looking for Foxie."

"I'll help," said Red. "Where should we look, Jack?"

I didn't know. I'd expected Foxie to be in the tent. Maybe the onions had confused his **sniffer**? That wouldn't stop Foxie. Before I could say so, I heard a familiar voice.

"Lordie? Lordeeeee!"

"Got to go," said Red. "Caterina Smith is calling. Perhaps she has saved me a sausage."

After Red left, I checked the other tents in search of Foxie. There were no more sausages, but I found some deluxe doghouses, and a pile of baskets. Then I detected bins of dog toys.

I was just wondering if Sarge and I might get a new **squeaker bone**, when Foxie sneaked behind the green tent.

"Halt!" I yipped. "Auntie Tidge
wants you."

"I'm doing something **im-paw-tant**."

"Howling about sausages is not
im-paw-tant," I said. Then I realized
Foxie *wasn't* howling now. He was
sneaking.

"There are sausage thieves around.
I am **staking out** this tent to guard
the sausages Caterina Smith stole
from Auntie Tidge," Foxie said.

"Caterina Smith didn't *steal* sausages," I said. "No one stole sausages. There has been no crime after all."

"She did so steal sausages," said Foxie. "Jack and Jill Johnson have them now. My sausages must be protected. There is going to be another theft!"

Jack's Glossary

Jack-attack. *Growling and biting and worrying at trouser legs. Very loud. Quite harmless.*

Pointed. *Clever dogs use their noses to point to things.*

Jack's Glossary

Sniffer. *A dog's nose in tracking mode. Only Jack Russell terriers have super-sniffers.*

Squeaker bone. *Item for exercising teeth. Not to be confused with a toy.*

Im-paw-tant. *Important, for dogs.*

Stakeout. *Hiding and watching for pupetrators (see next chapter).*

 Skulldoggery

"There haven't been *any* thefts," I said.
"We made a mistake."

"I saw a bonehead sneak under
the wall," said Foxie. "What does that
say to you?"

"A sneaking bonehead is certainly
up to **skulldoggery**," I agreed.

"Exactly," said Foxie. "That's why I
set up this stakeout. Those sausages
are going to disappear very soon."

"A bonehead won't get away with
it," I objected. "They aren't smart
enough."

"The bonehead isn't the only dog involved. There's a smaller dog as well," explained Foxie. "He is *very* smart. It's a cunning plan, Jack. One dog distracts Jack and Jill Johnson, while the other prepares to remove the sausages."

I was amazed. While I had looked for Foxie, Foxie had staked out a crime-scene-to-be.

"When is this theft going down?" I asked. "Who else is a witness? How many **pupetrators** are involved?"

"Don't in-terrier-gate *me*," snapped Foxie. "In-terrier-gate the bonehead in the bonnet! These sausages must be saved!"

"Can you give a description of the other dog?"

"It's a smart, handsome, small dog," said Foxie.

"Stay here, then," I ordered. "I'll set up a stakeout near the door. These **canine criminals** can't get past two of us."

I knew the smaller pupetrator would be more difficult to catch, so I hid just outside the entrance to the tent. I listed suspects in my head. Foxie had said it was a small dog. This cut out setters, spaniels, Dalmatians, and Labradors.

Right, Jack, I asked myself. What small dog *would* steal sausages?

That was easy. Any dog that was not respectable.

That left a pawful lot of suspects.

Right, Jack, I thought. What small dog *could* steal sausages?

Before I could answer that, Polly Smote trotted past. It certainly wasn't her.

"Out you go, Polly," said Jill Johnson from inside the tent.

Polly trotted out again. "What do you want, Jack Russell?"

"I'm working on a case," I said. "Someone is about to steal sausages. When I catch the pupetrator I shall bark for backup."

"I'm not your pupetrator. Maybe it's him." Polly pointed her long dachshund nose at a Dalmatian. It was creeping on its belly.

"That's not the thief," I said. "Jill Johnson will spot that dog easily."

"Out, darned Spot!" said Jill Johnson loudly.

"Told you," I said. "Besides, Dalmatians are not *small* dogs."

"Who says the pupetrator is a small dog?" Polly wanted to know.

"Foxie. He has a stakeout around the back," I said.

"How could a small dog reach them?" Polly pointed at the sausage boxes.

"A clever small dog could do it," I

said. I crawled forward to look up at the boxes. "I could jack-jump that high. I suspect the pupetrator may be a terrier. Terriers are quick and clever."

I demonstrated my best jack-jump for Polly.

"I can see you, Jack Russell!" said Jill Johnson. She wagged her tongs at me. "Shoo, both of you!"

I backed away.

"Go!" said Jill Johnson.

Three spaniels wearing socks slunk out of the tent.

Polly and I moved to a stakeout behind the canvas flap, where Jill Johnson could not see us.

"You're barking up the wrong tree here," said Polly. "No dog is stealing sausages."

Just then, the bonehead in the bonnet burrowed out under the side of the tent. "Halt in the name of the paw!" I snapped. "Polly! Crime in progress! Back me up!"

I leapt forward to make an arrest.

Jack's Glossary

Skulldoggery. *Bad things concerning dogs.*

Pupetrator. *A criminal who happens to be a pup or a dog, or who does things to dogs.*

Canine criminals. *Bad dogs.*

Spreading the Word

The bonehead snarled. "I see a terrier toothpick." (That's what boneheads always say.)

"I see a bonehead in a bonnet." It was the first time I'd had a chance to say *that*.

"What do you want, toothpick?"

"I'm arresting you on suspicion of sausage theft," I said.

"Not guilty," said the bonehead.

"We have a situation, bonehead. Sausages are being stolen from this tent."

"Not guilty," repeated the bonehead.

"You can't deny you were crawling under the side of the tent with intent to steal."

"Of paws I don't deny it. Any bonehead will crawl after sausages."

"And you haven't succeeded?" I demanded.

"Not a sausage," said the bonehead.

Polly sniffed with her long dachshund nose. "He's telling the

truth, Jack. He's been eating corn dogs and pie, not sausages."

I was about to release the bonehead from custody, when I remembered something. "You admit to attempted theft," I said. "Who is your partner in crime?"

The bonehead growled. "Boneheads don't have partners. We have **henchdogs**."

"Who is your henchdog, then?"

The bonehead showed his fangs. Some dogs would have laughed at his bonnet. I am not like that. I told the bonehead he was **pawfectly** free to go.

"That's silly, Jack Russell," said Polly. "What bonehead would work with a small dog? Boneheads use small dogs as toothpicks."

She had a point.

Jack's Facts

A smart detective will always admit a mistake.
This is especially so if it is someone else's mistake.
Jack Russells are the smartest detectives around.
This is a fact.

"I think Foxie is lying," said Polly.

I went to Foxie's stakeout. Foxie was not there.

Why would Foxie lie? Did he want to arrest the small henchdog himself? *Was* there a henchdog?

Inside the tent, I heard Jack Johnson tell Shuffle to go away.

"Jack? What are you doing here?"

I jack-jumped around. Foxie was peering out from under the tent wall.

"I'm looking for you!" I said.

"Did you arrest that bonehead?"

"He's innocent," I said. "What have *you* been doing?"

"I've been admiring a master sausage thief at work," said Foxie. "That dog is *so* smart!"

"Why haven't you barked for backup?" I asked.

"That dog is an artist," said Foxie. "He's working with a pug now. A while ago, it was a dachshund. Why not in-terrier-gate the pug, Jack?"

"I'd rather see this clever dog."

"OK," said Foxie. "Watch the

sausages, Jack. Bark for backup if you see the pupetrator."

I staked out the front of the tent and watched sausage boxes.

Jack and Jill Johnson kept telling me to go away. I ig-gnawed them. Foxie *must* be mistaken. A terrier *could* jack-jump to the sausage boxes, but Jack and Jill Johnson would notice.

"Jack, Jack!" Lord Red rushed right into the middle of my stakeout. "Foxie says a clever small dog is planning a sausage heist!"

"Hush!" I scolded. "Don't tell the world!"

Red's ears drooped. "I have to tell *everyone*! Foxie said so!"

"Oh, did he?" I snapped. "Just who is in charge of this Sausage Situation?"

"Foxie said *he* was," said Red.

"This is getting right out of paw," I growled.

Jack's Glossary

Henchdog. *A dog who is a partner in crime.*

Pawfectly. *Perfectly, only used for dogs.*

 # Pan-dog-monium

Before I could act, Shuffle wheezed into my stakeout.

Jack's Facts

If a Jack Russell terrier wheezes, it is sick.
If a pug wheezes, it is just being a pug.
That is a fact.

"Jack, a clever small dog is about to steal some sausages!" wheezed Shuffle. "I want to find that clever dog.

I'll ask him for some sausages."

"Yes!" chimed in Red. "I want to meet him, too. Can you detect him, Jack?"

"That's just what I'm doing!" I explained.

Red rushed away. "Clever dog!" I heard him calling. "Clever little dog! Where are you? Can I have a sausage?"

"**Bathwater!**" I said. "He's going to ruin everything!"

"If Red is getting sausages, I want sausages too," said Shuffle. "See you later, Jack."

I returned to Foxie's stakeout. "Are you out of your mind?" I asked. "Why did you tell Red and Shuffle about this clever small dog?"

"Why not? The more dogs on the job, the better!" said Foxie.

"All this fuss will alert the pupetrator!" I reminded him. "Too many dogs will get in one another's way when the crime goes down."

"Jack!" Ralf Boxer bounced under my belly and nipped my toe. "Shuffle says a clever dog will give everyone sausages. He doesn't know who it is. I want to know."

"We *all* want to know," I growled. There was something pawfully wrong here.

Think, Jack! I told myself. *I* am clever. So is Jill Russell. So is Polly Smote.

I checked off the small, clever dogs I knew in Doggeroo. None of them was a thief.

"It is a very clever Chihuahua," yapped Ralf Boxer. "We small dogs never get the recognition we deserve!"

"When you find out, tell, Jack," said Foxie. "Spread the word! This situation could break any second!"

After Ralf Boxer had gone, the Squekes appeared, yaffling for information.

"Stop it, Foxie," I growled. "Everything is getting out of paw!"

Foxie didn't answer. He pointed suddenly towards the dog-toy tent. "Sausages! Sausages! Sausages!" he yapped.

"Where? Where? Where?" yaffled the Squekes.

"Didn't you see?" yapped Foxie, darting across the grass. "There he goes! Stop that sausage dog!"

In seconds, all the dogs were barking as loudly as Foxie.

"There! Where?"

"The toy tent! See?"

"Where?"

"Catch that dog!"

"What dog?"

"A CLEVER DOG HAS TAKEN ALL THE SAUSAGES!"

The hunt was on. Dogs were everywhere, barking and passing on the news. People tripped over them and yelled. A pile of terriers leapt into a bin of rubber bones, and fifteen bouncy-balls hopped all over the ground.

Red pounced on one, and the three Squekes yaffled over a plastic squeaker chop.

Foxie rushed in circles, as if he was trying to catch his tail. He seemed to have gone crazy.

Jack and Jill Johnson raced out of the tent, waving their tongs.

"What on earth is going on?" asked Jill Johnson. "Is it a dog fight?"

"Not *a* dog fight," yelled Jack Johnson. "It's about twenty dog fights!"

"Watch out!" cried Gloria Smote, and tripped over Shuffle, who was biting into a dropped corn dog.

Jack Johnson tried to grab Foxie as he scooted by, but Foxie doubled back and vanished into the pile of dogs.

It was **pan-dog-monium**!

Red dropped the ball and galloped up to me. "Where's the clever sausage dog, Jack? Where?"

"Over here!" yapped Ralf Boxer.

I ran after Ralf Boxer. Jack and Jill Johnson ran after us, followed by Caterina Smith, Dora Barkins, Sarge and just about everyone else. The pan-dog-monium was getting worse.

There was going to be a terrier-able disaster if someone didn't take matters in paw. Sarge was doing his best, but Sarge is not a dog. This called for strong measures by a strong pack leader. And I knew just the dog for the job!

Jack's Glossary

Bathwater. *One of the worst swear words I know.*

Pan-dog-monium. *A lot of noise that involves dogs.*

"Stop in the Name of the Paw!"

Jack's Facts

Jack Russell terriers are not big dogs.
Occasionally this is a disadvantage.
A clever Jack can solve this problem
with ease.
This is a fact.

I jack-jumped onto the roof of the tallest deluxe doghouse, and surveyed the situation. Someone, or something, was at the bottom of this pan-dog-monium. I considered the dogs I knew. None of them had ever been mixed up with *this* kind of skulldoggery.

Maybe it was a dog I didn't know? I sniffed the air.

I couldn't detect any strange dog smells. Neither could I see any dogs I didn't know.

I was terrier-ably **paw-plexed** until I realized I couldn't see one I *did* know.

Where was Foxie?

Foxie *should* have been here. Surely he wanted to be in at the arrest of the clever sausage thief?

"Where's Foxie?" I yapped to Lord Red as he sailed by. Red didn't hear. He was still telling everyone about sausages and clever dogs.

I balanced on my hind legs on the

deluxe doghouse. I couldn't see Foxie. I even jack-jumped a few times. No Foxie.

I pricked my ears, but I couldn't hear Foxie.

Quickly, I made a nose map.

Jack's map:

1. Lots of dogs.

2. Lots of people.

3. Foxie.

4. Sausages.

5. Onions.

I turned around slowly, sniff-sniffing until I got a good direction. Aha! The scent of Foxie was coming from the tent.

The sausage thief must have returned to the tent under cover of the pan-dog-monium. Foxie must have seen the pupetrator and tracked it back to the tent. I had to get there quickly, to make the arrest!

I jack-jumped off the deluxe doghouse, and hit something hairy on the way down. Lord Red yelped.

"I'm under attack! I'm being dognapped! Help, Jack!"

I bounced to my feet. No time to stop and talk to Red now. The case was about to break wide open.

I dove under Red's belly, and raced back towards the tent.

Ralf Boxer got in my way, but I jumped over him, and nearly landed on Shuffle.

"I've been mugged!" snuffled Shuffle. He yelped. Ralf Boxer had bitten his toe.

I dashed past my old stakeout and through the entrance of the tent, then skidded to a halt.

I knew just what I would see …
and there it was. A box of sausages
had been knocked off the table. It had
burst open on the ground.

Sausages were hanging out in
long, delicious strings.

Foxie squatted on a pile of
buttered bread, guzzling and feasting.

"Stop in the name of the paw!" I commanded.

My pal went right on guzzling.

"Foxie, STOP!" I barked. "You're letting the pupetrator get away!"

I could see just what had happened. Foxie had come to make an arrest, but the sight of the sausages had been too much for him. He had stopped for a snack while the pupetrator made his getaway.

"Foxie!" I snapped. "Pull yourself together! Which way did he go?"

Foxie burped, and ate another sausage.

"What are you *doing*?" I demanded.

"Eating my sausages," said Foxie through a mouthful. "Go away, Jack."

Jack's Glossary

Paw-plexed. *Perplexed and puzzled.*

Foxie Logic

That was almost the end of the Sausage Situation.

Since Foxie wouldn't listen to reason, I had a quick **jack-snack** and then barked for backup. Jack and Jill Johnson and Sarge came back, but Foxie had already eaten a dozen sausages.

Auntie Tidge had to take him home.

I enjoyed the rest of Dog and Sausage Day. Lord Red was right. When there is no **skulldoggerer** around, games and sausages are fun!

Sarge and I got to judge the pet parade. The bonehead in the bonnet won. His prize was a day at a dog spa.

"Good!" he said. "What's a dog spa?"

"Soap," I said. "Shampooch. Clippers."

The bonehead snarled. "I'll get you for this, toothpick!"

All the runners-up got a chew toy and a sausage, and afterwards, Sarge bought me a new squeaker bone.

Foxie was quite sick that night, so I left the official in-terrier-gation until the next day.

"What was all that **dogwash** about a clever small dog heisting sausages?" I demanded.

"It wasn't dogwash. It was *true*," said Foxie. His belly rumbled, and he groaned.

"No Foxie. *You* took the sausages. There never was a clever small dog in the case. You made that up."

Foxie growled at me. "I am a clever dog. I am a small dog. And I wasn't stealing. I was *preventing* a crime."

He hiccuped.

"Foxie ... "

"Look," said Foxie. "Those sausages were on the ground in my terrier-tory. That makes them rightfully mine. The only way I could keep them safe was by eating them."

He burped.

"You said the bonehead was working with you. Then you said you were working with a pug and a dachshund."

"Of paws!" said Foxie. "They all

distracted the criminals while I laid
my clever plot."

"But there were no criminals!" I
snapped. "Except for you!"

"Jack and Jill Johnson had my
sausages. That makes them criminals."

I stared at my pal. Foxie? Clever?
Maybe he was, but I couldn't follow
his logic.

Just then, Auntie Tidge came out of the house, carrying a bowl. "Foxie-woxie … I have some leftover sausages here. Would you like some for dinner?"

Foxie looked sick. "Go away," he said to me.

I followed Auntie Tidge back into her kitchen. I did the paw thing and wagged my tail.

Auntie Tidge gave me the sausages and I cleaned them up.

I do like to help Auntie Tidge.

I was just polishing the bowl when Sarge called to say it was time to pay my visit to Jill Russell.

I said goodbye to Auntie Tidge and raced home.

"I'll eat my sausages tomorrow," said Foxie as I passed him.

"Too late," I said. "They're all gone."

The last thing I heard as I squeezed through my own dogdoor was Foxie howling.

"I'll get you for this, Jack Russell!"

Jack's Glossary

Jack-snack. *A snack for a Jack.*

Skulldoggerer. *Someone who does something bad concerning dogs.*

Dogwash. *Rubbish!*

About the Authors

Darrel and Sally Odgers live in Tasmania with their Jack Russell terriers, Tess, Trump, Pipwen, Jeanie and Preacher, who compete to take them for walks. They enjoy walks, because that's when they plan their stories. They toss ideas around and pick the best. They are also the authors of the popular *Pet Vet* series.